Over on a Mountain

Somewhere in the World

By Marianne Berkes

Illustrated by Jill Dubin

Dawn Publications

Over on a mountain
Grazing in the morning sun,
Lived a wooly mother llama
And her little *cria* one.

"Roll," said the mother.
"I roll," said the one.
So they rolled in the dirt
Grazing in the morning sun.

Over on a mountain
Where the bamboo grew,
Lived a giant mother panda
And her little *cubs* two.

"Eat," said the mother.
"We eat," said the two.
So they ate, ate, and ate
Where the bamboo grew.

ASIA

Minshan Mtns.

Over on a mountain
Near an evergreen tree,
Lived a mother Alpine ibex
And her little *kids* three.

"Climb," said the mother.
"We climb," said the three.
So they climbed on a ledge
Near an evergreen tree.

EUROPE

Alps

Over on a mountain
Where they often would snore,
Lived a stocky mother wombat
And her little *joeys* four.

"Sleep," said the mother.
"We sleep," said the four.
So they slept in their burrow
Where they often would snore.

AUSTRALIA

Blue Mtns.

Over on a mountain
Where leaves and berries thrive,
Lived a shy mother gorilla
And her little *babies* five.

"Forage," said the mother.
"We forage," said the five.
So they foraged in a forest
Where leaves and berries thrive.

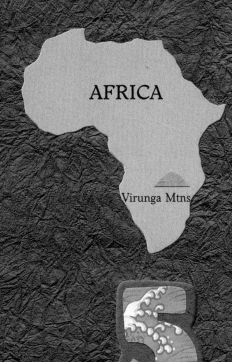

AFRICA

Virunga Mtns

Over on a mountain
Where they did gymnastics,
Lived a mother snow leopard
And her little *cubs* six.

"Leap," said the mother.
"We leap," said the six.
So they leaped on the rocks
Where they did gymnastics.

ASIA

Himalayan Mtns.

Over on a mountain
Gliding up toward heaven,
Lived a huge mother eagle
And her little *eaglets* seven.

"Soar," said the mother.
"We soar," said the seven.
So they soared with the wind
Gliding up toward heaven.

Alaska Range

NORTH
AMERICA

7

Over on a mountain
Where she knew how to wait,
Lived a mother mountain lion
And her little *cubs* eight.

"Pounce," said the mother.
"We pounce," said the eight.
So they pounced on their prey
Where they knew how to wait.

NORTH AMERICA

Rocky Mtns.

Over on a mountain
Where the sun does shine
Lived a friendly mother yak
And her little *calves* nine.

"Huddle," said the mother.
"We huddle," said the nine.
So they huddled in the cold
Where the sun does shine.

ASIA

Altai Mtns.

Over on a mountain
With his mate, a female "hen,"
Lived a father emperor penguin
And his little *chicks* ten.

"Waddle," said the father.
"We waddle," said the ten.
So they waddled on the ice
With his mate, a female "hen."

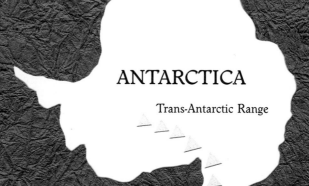

ANTARCTICA

Trans-Antarctic Range

Alaska Range

NORTH
AMERICA

Rocky Mtns.

EUROPE

Alps

AFRICA

Virunga Mtns.

SOUTH
AMERICA

Andes Mtns.

ANTARCTICA

ASIA

Altai Mtns.

Minshan Mtns.

Himalayan Mtns.

AUSTRALIA

Blue Mtns.

Trans-Antarctic Range

Over on a mountain
Living wild, living free,
As you look upon each page
Count the babies that you see.

Some live on the mountains
That are in the USA.
Others live on continents
Very far away.

Once you've named the continents
Then spy with your eyes,
To find a hidden creature—
Every page has a surprise!

Fact or Fiction?

In this variation of the popular old song, "Over in the Meadow," all the mountain animals actually behave as they have been portrayed. Snow leopards *leap*, bald eagles *soar* and penguins *waddle*. That's a fact! But do they have the number of babies as in this rhyme? No! That is fiction. Emperor penguins only have one chick, not ten as in this story, and mountain gorillas usually have just one baby, not five. Do the babies live in the mountains shown in this book? Yes, they live where shown on the map, but sometimes live in other places too.

Baby animals are cared for in different ways. Male snow leopards take no part in raising or protecting their cubs. But both mother and father eagle take care of their eaglets (usually one to three babies) until they are no longer helpless. And penguin males play a very unusual and important part in the birthing process. Nature has very different ways of ensuring the survival of different species.

Mountain Facts

Mountains can be found on all seven continents. They rise above the surrounding land, usually in the form of a peak. Mountain ranges are formed very slowly by movements of the Earth's crust. The height of a mountain is usually measured as the distance above sea level. The tallest mountain in the world *above sea level* is Mt. Everest at 8,848 meters.

Almost every country in the world uses the *metric system*, measuring in *meters*, not *feet*. In the United States, however, Mt. Everest would be 29,029 feet *above sea level*. But if you were to measure from the *base* of a mountain (which may be on the floor of the ocean) to the top, the highest mountain would not be Mt. Everest — it's Mauna Kea in Hawaii, at 10,100 meters or 33,100 feet.

In general, the higher you go, the colder it is. To say this another way, temperature decreases as elevation increases — about 5.4 degrees for every 1000 feet gained in elevation. For example, if the temperature is 90 degrees F. at the base of a mountain, it will be approximately 74 degrees F. if you go 3000 feet up the mountain. So is every high mountain a very cold place? Well, not necessarily — temperature also depends on where in the world the mountain is. A high mountain near the equator, where it is generally hot, will be a lot warmer than an equally high mountain in Antarctica or Alaska!

All of this is very important because animals depend on plants for food, and few plants are *hardy* enough to grow at very high altitudes. Many animals will live high on mountains during the summer, but move downhill during the winter to find food.

Who Are the "Hidden" Mountain Animals?

CHINCHILLAS are rodents that are slightly larger than ground squirrels. They live together in colonies, making their dens in burrows and among rocks. Chinchillas have soft dense fur to protect them from the cold weather of the high Andes Mountains.

GOLDEN EAGLES are raptors with beautiful gold feathers on the backs of their heads. They can be found in arid areas where there is little water, pursuing small mammals with their powerful beaks and talons, unlike bald eagles which are found near water and mainly hunt fish.

MARMOTS are large squirrels that live in burrows in mountainous areas such as the Alps. They are very social and use loud whistles to communicate with each other. They are herbivores that eat mainly grasses, lichens, and mosses.

SUGAR GLIDERS are small tree-dwelling marsupials with fox-like ears and big eyes. They have two thin flaps of skin that span from the fifth finger to the first toe on each side of the body, which allows them to glide through the air from tree to tree.

GREY-THROATED BARBETS are plump-looking solitary birds with large heads. They can be found in mountainous areas where they feed on fruit. They also eat a wide range of insects including ants and beetles.

JUMPING SPIDERS eat glacier fleas and springtails who have, in turn, eaten tiny bits of vegetation and pollen blown up to the Himalayas from many miles away. They spend the night frozen, waiting for heat from the sun to revive them in the daytime when they jump and scavenge for food.

MOOSE are the largest members of the deer family. They are strong runners with hoofed feet and long legs. Only the males (bulls) have antlers which drop off each year and regrow the following year. The biggest moose antlers in North America come from Alaska and the Yukon Territory.

BIGHORN SHEEP are hoofed mammals named for their large horns. They are closely related to goats and gather in large herds most of the year. Bighorn sheep live in mountain ranges from the Rocky Mountains in Colorado to southern Canada.

MOUNTAIN APOLLO BUTTERFLIES live on steep-sided slopes of high altitude mountains and tolerate a changing climate of dry summers and cold, snowy winters. This beautiful white butterfly is decorated with "eye" spots and shiny wings with transparent edges.

ARCTIC TERNS are the champion long-distance travelers of the animal world, traveling over 20,000 miles each year. When days grow shorter in the Arctic, they fly to Antarctica where summer is just starting so they can live in almost constant sunshine all through the year.

About the Animals in the Story

LLAMAS (pronounced "yamas") are wooly mammals related to camels. Llamas are used as pack animals. They have been helping people carry things across the **Andes Mountains** in South America for thousands of years. Llamas are alert and curious with keen senses of smell, hearing, and sight. They are herbivores—they eat mostly grasses and plant material. They like to *roll* in the dirt, taking dust baths that help maintain their fluffy wool coats. Baby llamas are called **crias**.

PANDAS are giant Chinese bears that have lived for several million years in the bamboo forests of five mountain ranges in central China, including the **Mishan Mountains**. Different from other bears, they have cat-like eyes and front paws with clawed fingers that grasp bamboo shoots and leaves, which they *eat* all day long. They use their powerful jaws and strong teeth to crush the tough bamboo into bits. Because bamboo is very low in nutrition, pandas need to consume about 40 pounds of it every day. Young pandas are called **cubs**.

The ALPINE IBEX is a kind of wild goat that lives among the forests and high rocky areas of the **European Alps**. They *climb* steep slopes to feed on grass and flowers that grow in meadows or among the rocks. They also eat lichens and mosses that grow on stones. The rocky ledges protect them from predators. In the winter, when there is lots of snow, they move to steep slopes where snow cannot pile up. Baby wild goats are called **kids**. Both male and females have horns.

WOMBATS live in underground burrows in the **Blue Mountains** of Australia. They have flat, wide paws with long, curved claws. As marsupials, their pouch is distinctive because it opens facing the mother's back legs. This prevents dirt from covering her baby while the mother is digging. The **joey** stays in the pouch until it can walk on its own. Wombats are nocturnal (active at night), when they eat grasses, leaves, and roots. They spend the day in the sleeping chamber of their burrow on their backs with their legs in the air, often *snoring* as they sleep.

MOUNTAIN GORILLAS are large, shy apes with thick fur that keeps them warm in the **Virunga Mountains** of Africa. They live in bands of six or seven with the adult male (silverback) heading the group. Mostly they eat leaves, fruit, and occasionally termites and ants. They *forage* for food during the day and sleep at night in bowl-shaped "nests" made out of leaves. The mother shares a nest with her nursing **baby** and nurtures it for three or four years. Females have one baby at a time. Mountain gorillas are on the verge of extinction; only about 600 of them remain.

SNOW LEOPARDS are athletic wild cats that live in the very high, cold **Himalayan Mountains**, mostly in the Tibet area of China. Their ears are small, which helps them retain body heat. Their large paws act as snowshoes; their long furry tails help them balance on rocky terrain. Snow leopards are carnivores that primarily hunt wild sheep and goats, but also ambush unsuspecting smaller animals. They can *leap* up to 30 feet—six times their body length—with their powerful hind legs. The mother usually gives birth to one to five **cubs** that are blind and helpless at birth and already have a thick coat of fur.

BALD EAGLES aren't really bald. They got that name because their white-feathered heads contrast with their brown bodies and wings. Female eagles are larger than males. Bald eagles are usually found near water abundant with fish, although they also capture other animals with their powerful talons. About half of the world's bald eagles live in Alaska, including the **Alaska Range**, but they can also be found throughout most of North America. Bald eagles *soar* using rising currents of warm air ("thermals") or up-drafts generated by terrain such as mountain slopes. Baby eagles are called **eaglets**.

MOUNTAIN LIONS are fierce, slender cats that hunt both day and night. Excellent jumpers and climbers, they often stalk their prey and ambush it by leaping from a tree. In the **Rocky Mountains** of North America they kill larger animals by *pouncing* on their backs and breaking their necks. These fast, solitary carnivores can reach speeds of 40 miles per hour as they chase prey such as deer. Female mountain lions have a special call to let males know they are ready to mate. After they do, the male goes his separate way and takes no part in raising the litter of one to three **cubs** that are born in a protected den.

YAKS are massive, shaggy-haired mammals who live high in the **Altai Mountains** of Central Asia, where there is lots of sunshine. It's the elevation that makes this place so cold and windy. But the wild yaks' dense fur keeps in body heat so they can live in temperatures of -40 degrees F. They gather in large herds and *huddle* together to protect themselves from the cold and from predators, with their young **calves** in the center. Yaks were domesticated hundreds of years ago to pull heavy loads through mountain passes. Like other species of cow, they are herbivores and graze on grasses and wild flowers. In winter they use their dense horns to break through snow to eat the plants beneath.

EMPEROR PENGUINS are birds that cannot fly. They are great swimmers, however, and spend most of their lives at sea. Many live on Antarctic pack ice in colonies at the base of the **Transantarctic Mountains** that stretch across the continent. During the coldest time of the year the female lays a single egg and the male incubates it for about 70 days, balancing it on his feet under a warm flap of skin called a "brood pouch." Meanwhile the female finds krill, squid, and fish in the ocean for her family, and eventually *waddles* her way back on the ice to feed her **chick**. Penguins waddle because their feet are set so far back on their bodies.

Tips from the Author

SING AND ACT out what each animal does: *roll, climb, soar, waddle,* and so on. Kids can also make masks of the animals and wear them as they enjoy the story. Use paper plates or see templates at: http://www.enchantedlearning.com/crafts/Mask.shtml

FUN WITH WORDS: Introduce vocabulary words in the story that younger children might not be familiar with, e.g. *cria, ibex, forage, prey, huddle, continent, equator, bamboo.* These words along with other more common ones can become "wordles" for older students to create "word clouds." Wordles are pictures made up from text that can be formatted with different fonts, sizes and colors into various layouts. See: http://resourcelinkbce.files.wordpress.com/2011/07/introduction-to-wordle.pdf

WHERE DO THEY LIVE? Using animal print-outs on the Enchanted Learning website, color and cut out each animal that is in the story. Draw or download a map of all the continents. Children can place their animals on the correct continent.

WHO AM I? Write two sentences describing an animal in this book, not mentioning which one it is, e.g., *I am different from other bears. I eat bamboo all day long.*

Construct an Attribute Chart

On the top horizontal sections of a grid enter category headings: "Continent," "Mountain Animal," and "Baby Name" for students to fill in after reading the story. Younger children can use a three-column chart, while older students can add other columns such as action (what they are doing in the story) what they eat (are they omnivores, carnivores or herbivores?) and are they nocturnal or diurnal?

Research the Mountains

Which mountain is the highest? Where is it located? What are some other mountains on that continent that are among the highest mountains in the world? How high is the highest mountain on each continent? You can draw a grid for this also, labeling the headings: Continent, Name of Mountain and Height. Older students may want to use two columns for the height (feet and meters).

Goin' to the Zoo. How about you?

Spend a day with family and friends observing zoo animals. It's such fun! And you can learn so much. Make a list of the animals in this book and see how many you can find at your zoo. What a great way to teach kids about respect for living creatures. Each time you go, you will share unique experiences that can last a lifetime.

Compare and Contrast

In a Venn Diagram, compare the hidden animal to the main animal on each page. How are they the same; how are they different? Describe their body parts, how they move, what they eat, sounds they make and so on. http://www.eduplace.com/graphicorganizer/pdf/venn.pdf

Discover more in books and on the internet

How Mountains Are Made by Kathleen Weidner Zoehfeld, Harper Collins

Mountain Animals by Francine Galko, Heinemann First Library

Mountain Animals (Saving Wildlife) by Sonya Newland Page, Franklin Watts Ltd.

A Day on the Mountain by Kevin Kurtz, Arbordale Publishing

http://www.mapsofworld.com/world-major-mountain.htm

http://www.sciencekids.co.nz/sciencefacts/topten/highestmountains.html

http://www.mountainprofessor.com/mountain-animals.html

http://www.enchantedlearning.com/coloring/

For more curriculum-connection activities, go to www.dawnpub.com and click on "Activities." Scroll to the cover of this book. You will find lesson plans aligned with Common Core and Next Generation Science Standards, along with reproducible bookmarks of the ten main animals in this book.

Tips from the Illustrator

In their natural habitat, animals use *camouflage* to blend into their environment. This is usually to protect themselves and their young from predators. Within each illustration the author has included a hidden animal for you to find. Some are easy to spot and some take a little more searching. As the illustrator, it's always a challenge for me to come up with ways to hide these creatures.

Just as color and texture help animals blend into their surrounding areas, I use the same idea in my illustrations. Each illustration is a collage using cut paper with pastel and colored pencil for details. I have a lot of wonderful papers with a wide range of colors and patterns and textures. I chose each paper carefully, thinking about how it will look when all of the pieces are put together.

When I'm planning the illustration, I keep the hidden element in mind. I try different papers to see what will help it blend into the background.

One morning when I went out to water my clematis plant, I noticed a newt perched on the edge of the planter. I took a picture of it before it scurried away. I used that photo to show how changing the background of a picture either makes the newt easy to see or much more difficult to spot.

The first photo is exactly as I took it. In the second photo, I isolated the newt so I could try different backgrounds. As you can see some of the backgrounds make the newt stand out and some make it very hard to find.

There are lots of hidden creatures in our environment—a green grasshopper on a blade of grass, a brown sparrow on a branch, or a gray bunny among the underbrush.

You may be able to see some hidden animals in your neighborhood if you keep still and look all around you.

Over on a Mountain

Sung to the tune "Over in the Meadow"

Traditional Tune
Words by Marianne Berkes

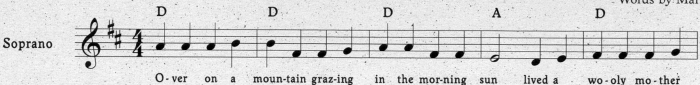

Soprano

O-ver on a moun-tain graz-ing in the mor-ning sun lived a wo-oly mo-ther

lla-ma and her lit-tle cri-a one "Roll," said the moth-er. "I roll," said the

one. So they rolled in the dirt____ gra-zing in the sum-mer sun.

2. Over on a mountain
   Where the bamboo grew,
   Lived a giant mother panda
   And her little cubs two.

   "Eat," said the mother.
   "We eat," said the two.
   So they ate, ate, and ate
   Where the bamboo grew.

3. Over on a mountain
   Near an evergreen tree,
   Lived a mother Alpine ibex
   And her little kids three.

   "Climb," said the mother.
   "We climb," said the three.
   So they climbed on a ledge
   Near an evergreen tree.

4. Over on a mountain
   Where they often would snore,
   Lived a stocky mother wombat
   And her little joeys four.

   "Sleep," said the mother.
   "We sleep," said the four.
   So they slept in their burrow
   Where they often would snore.

5. Over on a mountain
   Where leaves and berries thrive,
   Lived a shy mother gorilla
   And her little babies five.

   "Forage," said the mother.
   "We forage," said the five.
   So they foraged in a forest
   Where leaves and berries thrive.

6. Over on a mountain
   Where they did gymnastics,
   Lived a mother snow leopard
   And her little cubs six.

   "Leap," said the mother.
   "We leap," said the six.
   So they leaped on the rocks
   Where they did gymnastics.

7. Over on a mountain
   Gliding up toward heaven,
   Lived a huge mother eagle
   And her little eaglets seven.

   "Soar," said the mother.
   "We soar," said the seven.
   So they soared with the wind
   Gliding up toward heaven.

8. Over on a mountain
   Where she knew how to wait,
   Lived a mother mountain lion
   And her little cubs eight.

   "Pounce," said the mother.
   "We pounce," said the eight.
   So they pounced on their prey
   Where they knew how to wait.

9. Over on a mountain
   Where the sun does shine,
   Lived a friendly mother yak
   And her little calves nine.

   "Huddle," said the mother.
   "We huddle," said the nine.
   So they huddled in the cold
   Where the sun does shine.

10. Over on a mountain
    With his mate, a female "hen,"
    Lived a father emperor penguin
    And his little chicks ten.

    "Waddle," said the father.
    "We waddle," said the ten
    So they waddled on the ice
    With his mate, a female "hen."

MARIANNE BERKES has spent much of her life as a teacher, children's theater director and children's librarian. She knows how much children enjoy "interactive" stories and is an award-winning author of many entertaining and educational picture books that make a child's learning relevant. Reading, music and theater have been a constant in Marianne's life. Her books are also inspired by her love of nature. She hopes to open kids' eyes to the magic found in our natural world. Marianne now writes full time. She also visits schools and presents at literacy conferences nationwide. She is an energetic presenter who believes that "hands on" learning is fun. Her website is www.MarianneBerkes.com.

JILL DUBIN'S whimsical art has appeared in over 30 children's books. Her cut paper illustrations reflect her interest in combining color, pattern and texture. She grew up in Yonkers, New York, and graduated from Pratt Institute. She lives with her family in Atlanta, Georgia, including two dogs that do very little but with great enthusiasm. www.JillDubin.com

DEDICATIONS

For the Coblentz boys. May you always have a sense of wonder! — MB

In loving memory of my father, who climbed the heights and sailed the seas. — JD

Special thanks to Margaret Sims and students at Palmetto Elementary for the photo on the Tips from the Author page.

Copyright © 2015 Marianne Berkes

Illustrations copyright © 2015 Jill Dubin

Book design and computer production by
Patty Arnold, *Menagerie Design & Publishing*

DAWN PUBLICATIONS

12402 Bitney Springs Road
Nevada City, CA 95959
530-274-7775
nature@dawnpub.com

Library of Congress Cataloging-in-Publication Data

[Berkes, Marianne Collins.
Over on a mountain : somewhere in the world / by Marianne Berkes ; illustrated by Jill Dubin.
    pages cm
Summary: A counting book in rhyme that presents various animals and their offspring that dwell in high mountain environments, from a mother llama and her "little cria one" to an emperor penguin, his hen, and their "little chicks ten." Includes related facts and activities.
ISBN 978-1-58469-518-9 (hardback) -- ISBN 978-1-58469-519-6 (pbk.) [1. Stories in rhyme. 2. Mountain animals--Fiction. 3. Animals--Infancy--Fiction. 4. Counting.] I. Dubin, Jill, illustrator. II. Title.
PZ8.3.B4557Owm 2015
[E]--dc23

                                        2014031422]

Manufactured by Regent Publishing Services, Hong Kong
Printed December, 2014, in ShenZhen, Guangdong, China

10 9 8 7 6 5 4 3 2 1
First Edition

ALSO BY MARIANNE BERKES

Over in the Ocean: In a Coral Reef — With unique and outstanding style, this book portrays a vivid community of marine creatures. **Also available as an App!**

Over in the Jungle: A Rainforest Rhyme — As with "*Ocean,*" this book captures a rainforest teeming with remarkable animals. **Also available as an App!**

Over in the Forest: Come and Take a Peek — Follow the tracks of forest animals, but watch out for the skunk!

Over in the Arctic: Where the Cold Winds Blow — Another charming counting rhyme introduces creatures of the tundra.

Over in a River: Flowing Out to the Sea — Beavers, manatees and so many more animals help teach the geography of 10 great North American rivers.

Over in Australia: Amazing Animals Down Under — Australian animals are often unique, many with pouches for the babies. Such fun!

Going Around the Sun: Some Planetary Fun — Earth is part of a fascinating "family" of planets. Here's a glimpse of the "neighborhood."

Going Home: The Mystery of Animal Migration — Many animals migrate "home," often over great distances. A solid introduction to the phenomenon of migration.

Seashells by the Seashore — Kids discover, identify, and count twelve beautiful shells to give Grandma for her birthday.

The Swamp Where Gator Hides — Still as a log, only his watchful eyes can be seen. But when gator moves, he really moves! **Also available as an App!**

What's in the Garden? — Good food doesn't begin on a store shelf in a box. It comes from a garden bursting with life!

A FEW OTHER NATURE AWARENESS BOOKS FROM DAWN PUBLICATIONS

The Prairie That Nature Built — A romp above, below, and all around a beautiful and exciting habitat. There's nothing boring about a prairie!

Molly's Organic Farm is based on the true story of homeless cat that found herself in the wondrous world of an organic farm—seen through Molly's eyes.

Pitter and Patter — Take a ride with Pitter on a water cycle! You'll go through a watershed, down, around and up again. Oh, the places you'll go and the creatures you'll see. A water drop is a wonderfully adventurous thing to be!

On Kiki's Reef — A tiny baby sea turtle scrambles across the sandy beach and into the sea. Floating far out in the ocean, Kiki becomes a gentle giant and ends up with a fascinating community of creatures on a coral reef.

The "Mini-Habitat" Series — Field trips between covers! These books explore the small but fascinating "neighborhoods" of insects and other creatures to be found under rocks, around old logs, on flowers, near cattails, around cactuses, and in tidepools. See them all at http://www.dawnpub.com/our-store/habitats/.

The E-I-E-I-O Books follow the adventures of young Jo, granddaughter of Old MacDonald, as she discovers the delights of the pond, woods, and garden on Old MacDonald's farm. *Jo MacDonald Saw a Pond; Jo MacDonald Hiked in the Woods; and Jo MacDonald Had a Garden.* E–I–E–I–O!

Dawn Publications is dedicated to inspiring in children a deeper understanding and appreciation for all life on Earth. You can browse through our titles, download resources for teachers, and order at www.dawnpub.com or call 800-545-7475.